About the Author

Kayleigh Sorel is a first-time mom and debut children's book author living with her family in Albany, NY.

Her son, Johnny, was only two days old when COVID-19 shut down the state.

She wrote this book on her phone while rocking him to sleep one night.

About the Illustrator

Alicia van Zyl is an illustrator from beautiful South Africa. When she's not in Johannesburg, you'll find her on the streets of New York, probably eating a bagel.

Unless something like a global pandemic restricts all international travel, that is.

This is her 4th illustrated children's book.

This book is dedicated to my son, John.

In tough times, remember there will
always be a rainbow hiding somewhere.

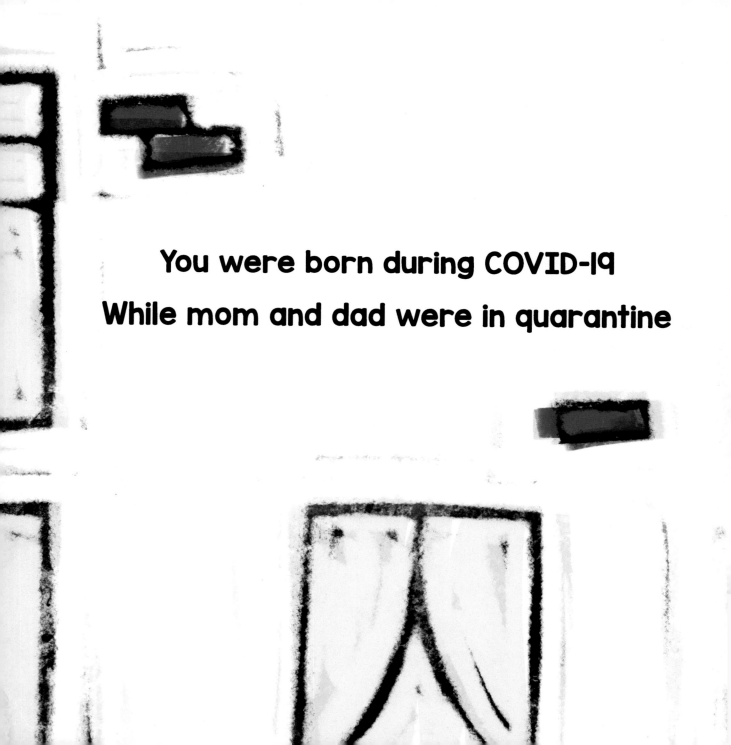

You were born during COVID-19

While mom and dad were in quarantine

Our hearts were full of excitement and fear

As your delivery date came near

We were off to the hospital
when that day arrived

And followed new rules, as advised

The nurses asked where we had been

They took our temperature as we walked in

The hospital told us no visitors allowed

But that didn't stop us from feeling proud

VISITORS

SNAC

PUSH

‖

Not ideal and second best

We announced your birth via text

14

When we brought you home,
everything felt new

We had no help but we finally had you

15

**Your grandparents' visits
were socially distanced**

All hugs and kisses were sadly resisted

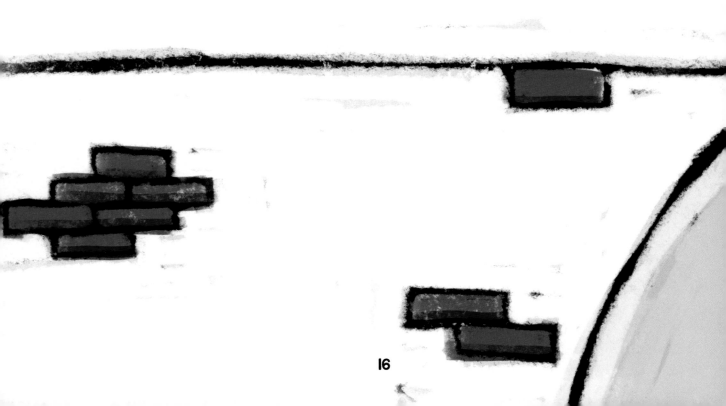

Video calling was used in place

Of moments which
would've been face-to-face

We stayed inside to stop the spread

And read many books while lying in bed

22

As we all fought back tears
trying to remain calm

You spent your days
cuddled up with mom

We followed the news every day

Eager to hear what
health experts would say

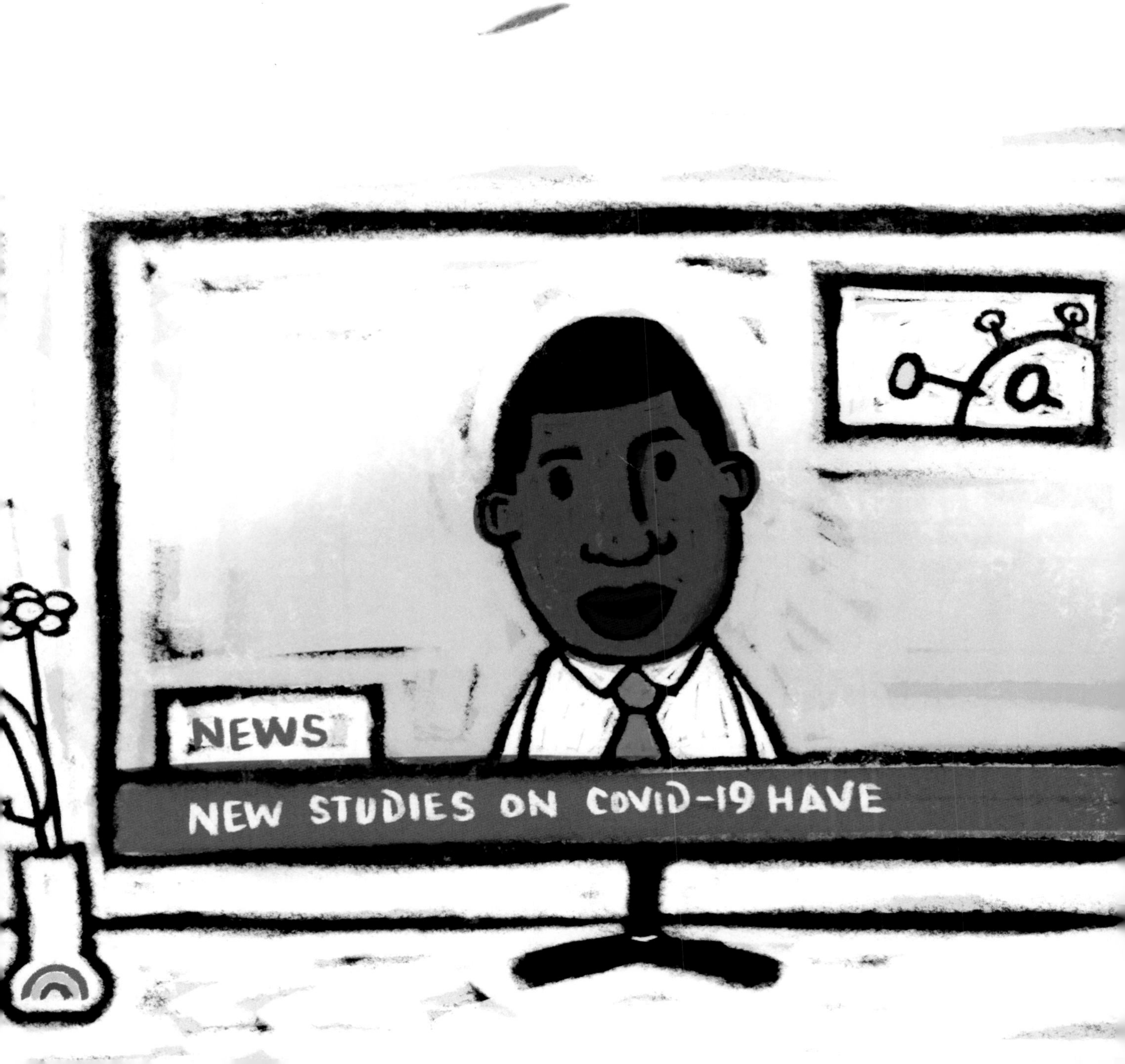
NEWS
NEW STUDIES ON COVID-19 HAVE

Most businesses had closed;
there was nowhere to roam

Everyone exclaimed "just stay home!"

Essential workers became our heroes

As we hoped infection rates
would drop to zero

Pizza delivery filled dad with glee

When our orders arrived contact-free

We always made sure to wear our masks

If we left our house for any task

At stores, toilet paper could not be found

We kept six feet apart from people around

Separated from cashiers with plexiglass

We reminded ourselves, this too shall pass

Anything that came home
was scrubbed clean

To keep us protected from COVID-19

We couldn't see where the virus would land

So we'd wash and wash and wash our hands

Nasal swabs were used at testing sites

42

For people to check if they were alright

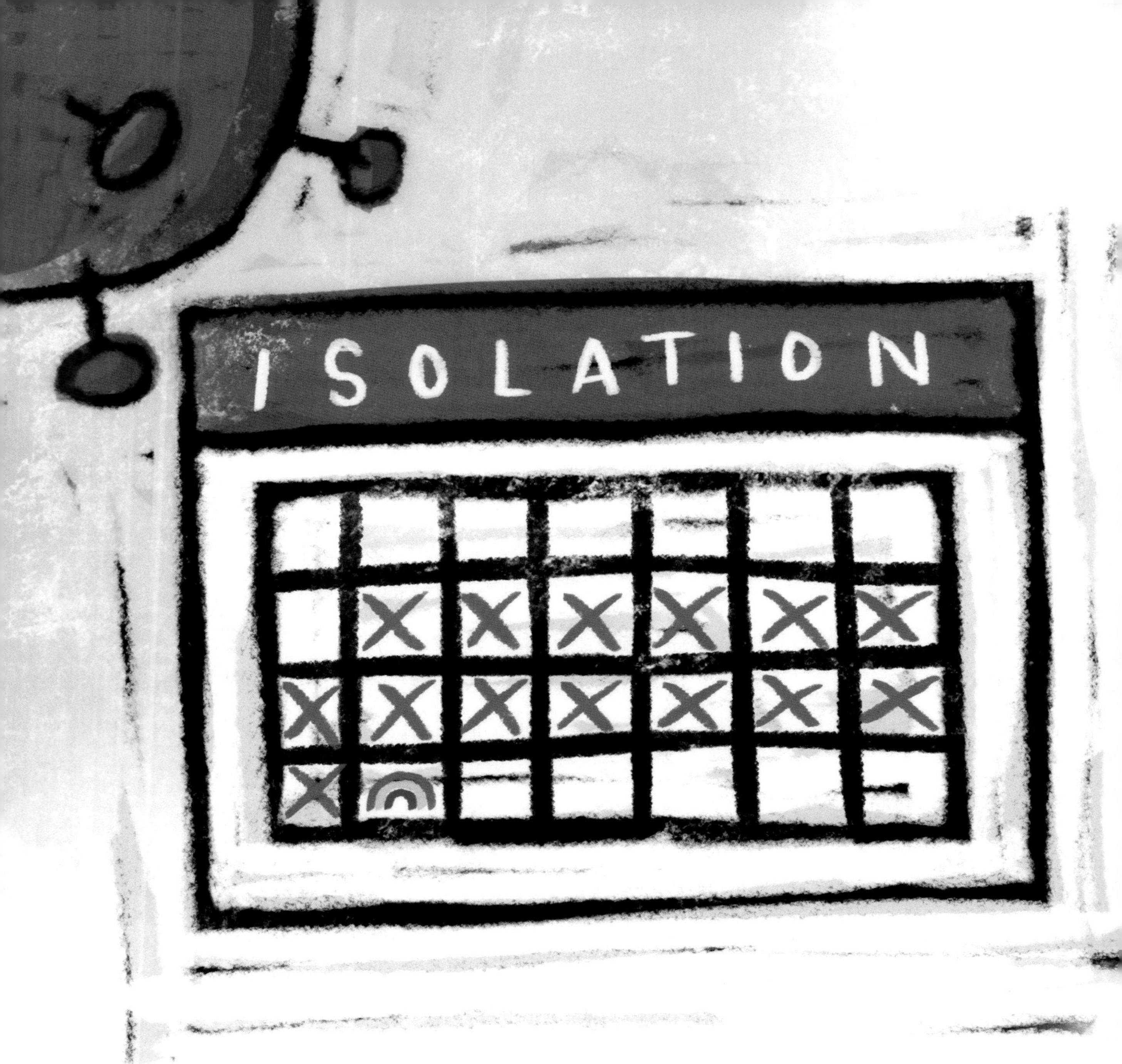
ISOLATION

If we had been exposed, we'd isolate

For two weeks
while the virus would incubate

All over the globe anxiety grew

But in our hearts, we knew we'd get through

WE WILL BE OKAY

We hit pause on concerts, parties,
and sporting events

Until the infection curve was bent

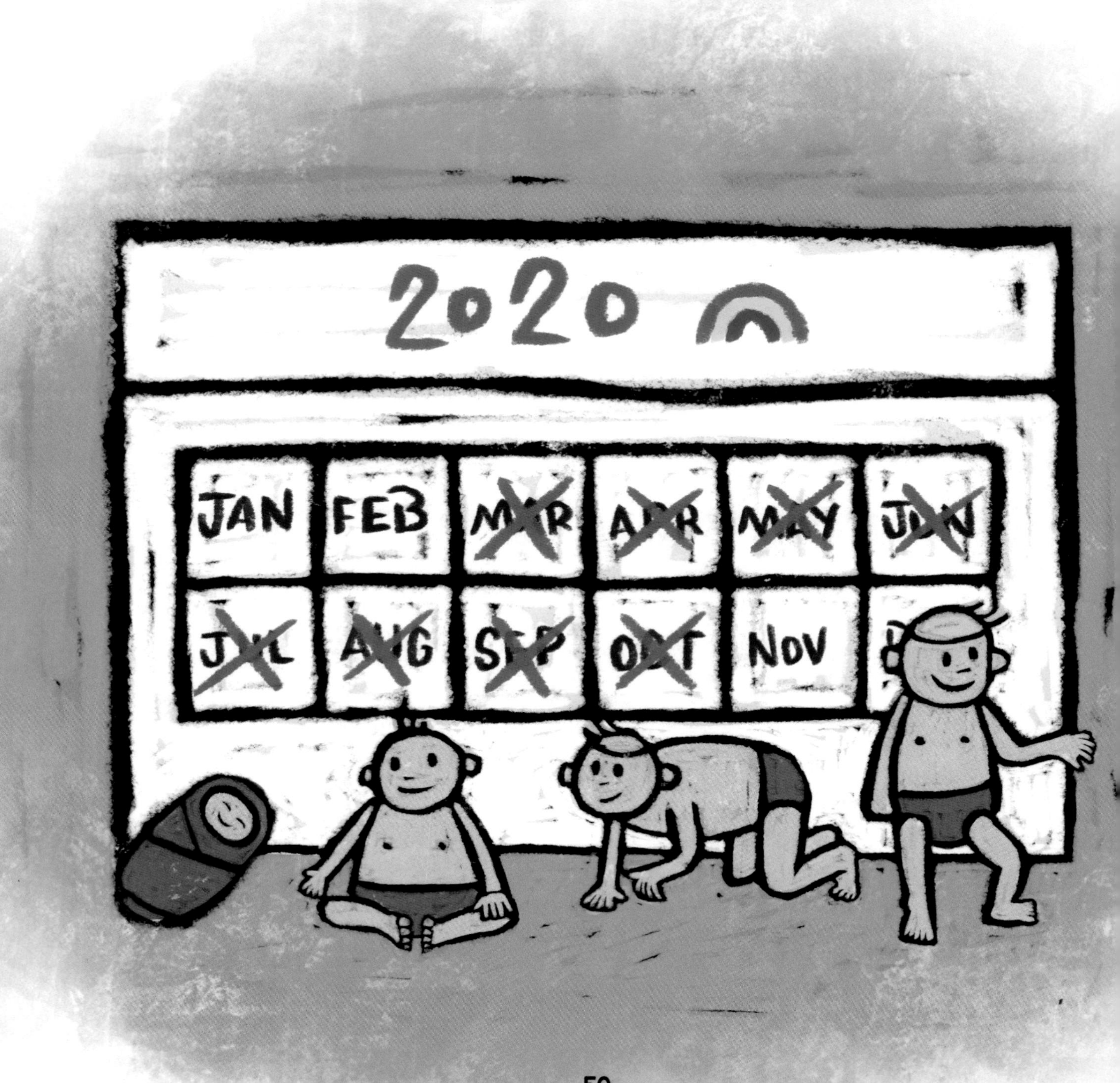
2020
JAN
FEB
NOV

And although it felt like time moved slow

We were happy at home to watch you grow

For this was only the beginning of your story

As cures were tested in the laboratory

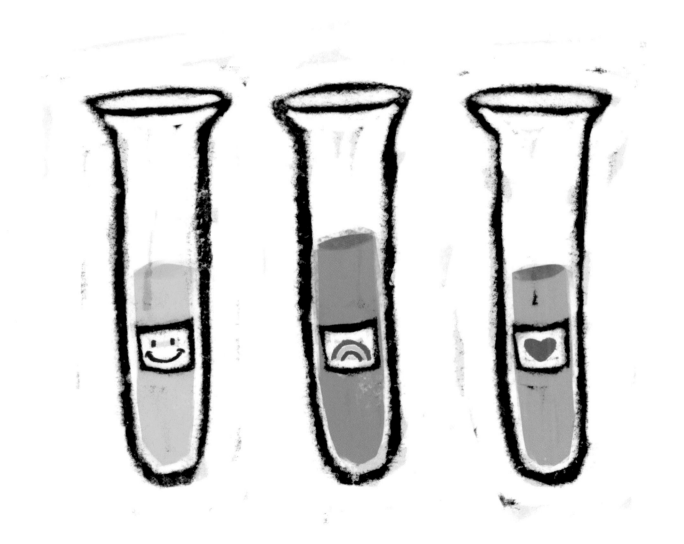

This pandemic created a new norm

And showed there can be rainbows
after a storm

Being born on the curve
was unexpected